I0519671

# WARNING

* * * * * * * * * * * * * * * * * * *

**WANT FREE COPIES OF MY BOOKS?**
Just visit my blog and download free copies of my books:
http://gideon-elliot.awesomeauthors.org/gideon-elliot/

## About the Publisher

**4Fun Publishing**, a member of **BLVNP Incorporated**, 340 S. Lemon #6200, Walnut CA 91789, info@blvnp.com / legal@blvnp.com

NOTE: Due to the highly emotional reaction of some people to works of erotic fiction, any email sent to the above address that contains foul language or religious references is automatically deleted by our anti-spam software and will not be seen. All other communications are welcome.

## DISCLAIMER

Please don't be stupid and kill yourself. This book is a work of FICTION. Do not try any new sexual practice that you find in this book. It is fiction and not to be confused with reality. Neither the author nor the publisher or its associates assume any responsibility for any loss, injury, death or legal consequences resulting from acting on the contents in this book. Every character in this book is over 18 years of age. The author's opinions are not to be construed as the opinions of the publisher. The material in this book is for entertainment purposes ONLY. Enjoy.

# My Fair Master

## 6-Book Box Set
## Gay Submission Erotica

By: Gideon Elliot

© Gideon Elliot 2015
ISBN: 978-1-62761-359-0

# MY FAIR MASTER

**Gay Submission Erotica**

# ABSINTHE

**GIDEON** **ELLIOT**

# Absinthe

In Antibes, just outside the walls of the old city, on the rue de Recherche, where boys lean against the wall wearing hardly more than their dark summer tans and wait for free-spending tourists to notice them, there's an absinthe bar in the basement of a shop that sells gourmet olive oil, scented vinegar, hand-crafted kitchen implements, mixed herbs, exotic pastas, and fancy soap during the day mostly to Americans and Germans who have a particular fondness for their kitchens and their bathrooms and the money to indulge it.

Looking like a van Gogh in yellow, blue, olive, and red, the assomoir is open after the shop upstairs has long been shut. Patrons come and leave through an ill-lit side entrance negotiating a flight of steep and twisting wooden steps. The pale and dirty stucco walls are coated with a red stain cast by the bare exit bulb stuck in the ceiling.

It is a quiet place with marble table tops and amber light bulbs. Water carafes with little spigots stand on chrome feet at the center of the tables. Sometimes some of the boys from outside lean against the bar nursing a drink and look blank, waiting for something to happen. I had taken to hanging out there nearly every night, either passing through just for one drink at the bar, or sometimes settling at one of the round tables to write or to sketch. Every now and then I'd gaze at the boys, admiring their youth, but since I never would consent to be a paying customer, none of them had eyes for me. And all I was left with was to wonder at their unreflecting inwardness.

As I was about to leave one evening in early August, hoping to take a walk along the ramparts overlooking the blue Mediterranean before complete nightfall, a young American, a good looking sunned and tousle-haired boy of around nineteen with sparkling, questing, needy eyes asked if he could sit down at my table.

"Sure," I said.

"I've seen you several times before this," he said, fastening his gaze upon me and catching mine in his.

I looked him over to see if I could recognize him, but had no recollection of having seen him before and was quite certain, given his good looks and lean but well-wrought frame apparent under his loose-hanging striped boatman shirt and faded jeans, that I would have if I had.

He smiled showing perfect teeth.

"You're not one of them," I said.

"What?"

"You're not one of the beach boys that hang around the street at night."

"No," he said. "I'm not."

"I can tell," I said.

"How?" he asked smiling. "By my eyes?"

"No," I said. "By the loose hang of your clothes."

He blushed.

"Who are you?" I said.

He told me his name.

"I've never seen you here before," I said. But I recognized his name. "Your father," I began, but he interrupted me.

"Yes," he said, and I knew all I needed to know and from politeness moved quickly away from the subject.

"Have we met?" I asked.

"I don't expect you'd have noticed me," he said modestly. "The last time I saw you, it was at the Picasso museum and you were totally absorbed by the de Stael exhibition. A few days before that, I saw you with a German boy having coffee in a café above the beach."

I winced. I remembered him.

He blushed when he added, "the only thing I think you could see was his eyes.

You both were gazing into each other's eyes to the exclusion of everything else."

"It happens," I said, "when I get lucky," I added, not without irony as we continued to mirror each other's gaze.

He registered the ambiguity but proceeded without letting it sabotage him.

"I want it to happen to me," he said, and blushed again, nevertheless looking straight at me.

"You do?" I said.

"With you," he said.

"With me," I said, quizzically.

"Yes," he said, determined not to be put off.

"Have you ever had absinthe?"

"I've only read about it," he said, shaking his head.

"Laurent," I said to the barman, signaling for a glass of La Muse Verte for the boy and a refill for me.

He brought them and I added water to each.

"You can put sugar in if you like," I said, "but I don't."

"Then I won't either," he said." I want to do things the way you do."

I looked at him.

"I have a sixth sense," he said, as we tilted our glasses towards each other, and our eyes began their slow embrace.

"I want you to make me your boy," he said. "I want to belong to you."

"Do you know what that means?" I said.

"I think I do," he said, "and I want to know how it feels." His voice was deep and sweet and slow.

I couldn't tell who was taking control of whom as we gazed into each other's eyes.

"Have you ever made love to a man?" I asked.

"No," he answered.

"Do you want to?"

"If the man is you," he said.

We stood beside each other on the old embankment above the beach and our eyes traced the vast blue stretch of the Mediterranean as it spread laterally and reached the infinitesimal depth of the horizon. Violet overspread everything as the sun fell. He took hold of my hand.

"I have imagined this since I first saw you," he said, and brought his lips near mine. "Please," he said, withdrawing a little and then kissing me again.

Our lips met and our breaths became indistinguishable from the on-coming night's translucent air.

"There's something unhealthy about this," I said, the next morning when he brought a small cup of coffee to my bedside.

"I don't understand," he said, frightened. "Didn't you like it?"

"Yes," I said, "I liked it very much."

And that was true. We had sustained a peak of excitement, we had become joined in an overwhelming pulsating vibration I had not known before and we had exploded with a profundity and breadth of sensation that shattered me completely but left me very happy. He had torn me apart and was luminous inside me, and I had penetrated his depths and was rooted there.

"But," I said, "I am not sure where all this is coming from."

"It's coming from us," he said.

I looked at him without saying anything.

"Why won't you believe that?" he said.

"I don't know," I said. "It's too simple."

"Don't be afraid," he said.

"Afraid?" I said.

"Of your happiness. I am not like the others."

"The others?" I said.

He blushed.

"What others?" I said.

"I know," he said, "but you need not worry."

"Worry about what?"

"That I will be like the others."

"What others?" I repeated.

"All the others: the ones who give you nothing and take everything away; the ones who stay with you until they are ready to go; the ones who stand around outside, beautiful, and empty, and waiting for something to bring them to life."

"And you are not waiting for that?"

He blushed again, but kept his gaze fixed on me. "No, I am not," he said. "Not now. Not anymore."

"Why?" I said.

"Because," he hesitated, "because I am here for as long as you want me to be."

"And then?"
He said nothing. He gazed into my eyes.

"I would like to hypnotize you."

"What?" I said.

"I would like to hypnotize you, put you in a trance?"

"Why?" I said dumfounded.

"So that I can make sure that you will always want me."

"We can go for a swim together," I said. "But then you have to let me work."

"Can we see each other again?" he asked. "Tonight?"

"I'll go to the absinthe bar around nine," I said.

"I'll meet you there," he said.

I was disappointed when he did not show up but not surprised. It seemed to be exactly what I had learned to expect. Nevertheless, it showed on my face.

"You can hide nothing," Laurent said, moving over to my table with his glass. "Tell me why you are so withdrawn tonight."

"More so than usual?"

"More so. Do not pretend."

"I've been stood up."

"A boy?"

"A young man."

"It is the same thing. One appreciates what they give. And then..."

"And then they go away."

"That is what you expect."

"That is what I expect."

"The expectation perhaps is the cause then, not the result."

"That my friend is cheap psychology entirely unworthy of you."

\*\*\*

**THE DUNGEON** of the fifteenth-century chateau whose ramparts stretched across the edge of the old city and served as a bulwark against the sea and, originally, as a look out and fortification was damp and lit by flaming torches planted in the crevices made by the fissures of damp rock and clay. Lavache stood with his feet spread and arms akimbo, bare-chested. Wearing only tight suede trousers that flared at the bottom over a pair of high-heeled pirate boots, he seemed, somehow more feminine than masculine despite his well-developed physique and dark, perfectly manicured mustache. A black leather patch covered his left eye, and a silver band encircled his right arm, caressing his biceps with a force that kept them in a state of constant tension. Little silver rings stood glinting from his pierced nipples. He held a coiled whip in his right hand and softly slapped it against his left palm as he spoke.

"The boy has been estranged from his father since he was fourteen. What was in your mind?"

"I thought, Sir," Ramsey stammered, afraid to lift his eyes.

"You thought?" Lavache goaded him.

"I thought that was all there was to bargain with, that his father still felt…"

"Felt! Warwick Fox Chamberlin runs a conglomerate empire and did not get the kind of wealth and power he commands by feeling."

"No, Sir. Only, I thought, if my master will permit me, that his father would be moved to forgive…"

The whip cracked without notice an inch to his left and he started.

"Will you make a fool of me?" Lavache said with calm ferocity. "Do you realize the trouble you have made? Do you understand that we are in real danger?"

\*\*\*

**JONATHAN SHOOK** his head as if casting off clouds of confusion. He had been drinking a coffee on a terrace overlooking the sea and reading Howards End. He was waiting for evening when he would go to meet Ben at the absinthe bar.

Now, there were chains around his wrists and ankles. As he sat up in an iron bed in a strange room with an aching head, he guessed what had happened.

He had been the victim of a trick. A man moving to a table behind him had bumped into him and made him spill his coffee just as he was bringing the cup to his lips. He remembered that. After an apology, he insisted on buying Jonathan another and went inside to get it himself.

He had spiked it. Of course! But why?

He remembered nothing else. Everything was fog.

Lavache entered the room. He was smiling. Jonathan thought he had never seen him before. But Lavache acted as if he knew him. He sat on the bed beside him and, as if he knew him, kissed him tenderly, seductively upon the mouth and pried his lips apart with his tongue.

Jonathan responded before he knew he was responding and grew hard and arched his back as Lavache played with his nipples.

He pulled away, frightened.

"Do you still insist on being chained to the bed?" Lavache said with an ironic, indecent smile after he broke the kiss. "Or have you had enough kink for one night, mon vieux?"

He was speaking English, and Jonathan was fluent in French, but he could make no sense of what this weirdly dressed stranger was talking about. As for the kiss, that had happened in a fog.

\*\*\*

**JONATHAN SURVEYED** the Mediterranean through dark sunglasses, still dazed. He was on his second cup of espresso. The dark period when he did not know what happened between the time he passed out until the time he awoke chained to the bed was haunting him with invisible images. But it had passed. He had been released. Just as arbitrarily it seemed as when he had been captured. He was puzzled.

A crumpled telegraph from his father lay in the ashtray. It had been waiting at his hotel. It made no sense to him, unless…unless what?

"What hell you trying do me?" Chamberlin had telegraphed his son. "Time grow up. No?"

\*\*\*

**INSIDE THE** assomoir I saw him before he saw me. He looked around, worried that I would be angry, that I would snub him, and that I would not be there. But I was there, absorbed by something no one else could see, scribbling in my notebook.

With an uncanny awareness, sensing the weight of the moment, I looked up. I saw him. Then our eyes met. I smiled. The boy trembled, painful longing in his gaze. He could not move. I stood up, approached him. Under the arch where he stood immobilized, I wrapped my arms around him.

One palm, cupped at the nape of his slender neck against the base of his skull, the other, holding the small of his muscled back, I brought him to me, pressed his cheek against my cheek, his chest against my chest, our hips and thighs together, too, and stood there gently rocking him, feeling the weight of his body dissolving into mine.

## End of the 1ˢᵗ book

End of the Preview

# Leather
# BOUNDARIES

## GIDEON ELLIOT

# Leather Boundaries

They sat late over espressos, transfixed by one another, talking about how much they were like each other.

Chance had thrown them together at Lincoln Center. They were seated next to each other at Wozzeck, complete strangers who knew at the first meeting of their eyes that they were made for each other. Each was delighted to find in the other not just the looks he'd have been happy to go home with if they'd crossed paths on Christopher Street, but a person like himself with similar interests, pursuits, fantasies.

They did not have to make conversation. They just flowed into each other.

When the café closed they left and walked through the warmth of the spring night pleased with each other and proud of the success of what they teasingly began to call their first date.

"You want to keep going, spend the night together?" Sandy said with a winning combination of shyness and spunk.

"Very much," Lex responded with a wink.

They took hold of each other's hands and on the dark street corner under the lamppost they faced each other and kissed themselves into eternity and then stumbled across the street as if they had become one being.

Lex's loft was all white and sparsely furnished. The few pieces in it lacked neither taste nor elegance. Everything was white -- furniture, walls, floor. But there were candles rather than electric light, casting upon everything in consequence an amber glow.

Lex wore a three-piece charcoal gray double-breasted Italian worsted suit with the faintest gray chalk stripe. His shirt was a white on white and his tie was a black, gray and silver striped silk. There was a matching breast pocket handkerchief and silver clocks adorned his black silk socks, which were held up under his trousers by silver garters. He wore gun metal black shoes of supple calf skin. His hair was long and almost black. Tonight it was combed close to his scalp and parted sharply on the right, highlighting his high cheekbones, square jaw, strong nose and white teeth. His eyes were wide set and of a penetrating gray. He was well-tanned, and to look at him you knew he had just spent a few weeks in the Caribbean.

Sandy was wearing a very dusty-hued three button brown suit with the palest sky blue chalk stripes. Like Lex, he favored a trouser pleated and cuffed, tight enough around the ass but flowing freely although not loosely, either, down the leg. His shirt, pocket handkerchief and socks were of the same celestial blue as the chalk stripe in his suit. So were his eyes. He wore a low boot of doe skin color with a slight heel. His hair was abundant and windblown and from its color you knew why from childhood "Justin" couldn't stick and everyone called him Sandy.

Lex poured armagnac into a snifter and put it to Sandy's lips.

"Drink," he said.

Sandy took a sip.

"Another," Lex said. "This time leave it on your lips."

He put the glass to his own lips. He covered Sandy's brandied lips with his own. Their lips parted. Their tongues caressed. They stretched more fully into each other with kisses that turned their souls upside down.

As they kissed, Sandy took hold of the perfectly fashioned Windsor knot at Lex's throat and gradually began to undo his tie until he had the two sides draping him like a scarf. Then he began to unbutton

Lex's shirt. Without stopping their cadenza of kisses Lex reached the brandy glass safely onto a side table, a white marble slab set on a white enameled art deco iron base. In his turn he loosened Sandy's tie and began unbuttoning his shirt until he saw the crescent of his white wifebeater. He pulled it up revealing Sandy's bare chest, and thrilled to feel that it was shaved. He molded his hand to the contours of the chest and kneaded his palm into the firm breasts. With his fingertips he traced the circles of the nipples and felt them stiffen. He lingered at the nipples, which he teased with alternating attention and frustration.

And then he went back to the lips, brushing kisses on them and then backing away repeatedly so that the more he fed Sandy with kisses the hungrier for them he became.

"I'm gonna get you so hot you're not gonna know what you're doing," he whispered to him before delivering the kiss he had been making Sandy swoon for by withholding it. "I'm going to turn you into my slave. You'd like that."

The arching and twisting of their bodies suggested the continuous ratcheting up of their energy and excitement.

Lex pulled himself back from a kiss just before it felt Sandy's lips, and instead whispered, "Beg for it. Say please."

"Please, Lex," Sandy said, and repeated it until the words became part of his breath. When his mouth was muffled with a kiss, he mouthed them inside the kiss he gave back.

\*\*\*

**IT WAS** with especial delight that Lex stared at Sandy as he lay stretched with the quilt thrown off him asleep in the candle light in only the black microfiber thong that Lex had given him to sleep in.

He was thinking before he began about what he was going to do to Sandy. He stared at him in wonderment. He was golden - and he was caught.

'This one's too good to let get away, or to risk letting him have his own way. I want full command.' He shook his head in agreement with his desire.

"You belong to me," he whispered with tenderness. "You will be a magnificent leather slave."

The sound of the words made him swoon.

He startled Sandy awake with a rough kiss and a fist around his scrotum. With his free arm he put weight on his chest, and said, in a whisper, "You please me."

Sandy raised himself from supine to nearly sitting by leaning on his elbows. His eyes were clear but with the expression of wistful devotion. He raised his head and pressed his lips to Lex's and clung to him with his tongue, feeling himself dissolve inside this man as he'd never felt himself do with anyone before. This man was his fulfillment.

From the side table Lex took a soft leather strap and gently started teasing Sandy with it.

Sandy opened his mouth deeper and surrendered to Lex's kisses. All that he could feel, throbbing in his blood and trembling on the membranes of his nerves, formulating itself in his mind and dancing on his skin was that he wanted this man inside him, that he wanted to give his body and his soul over to this man and serve him. He felt his muscles contracting with desire, and deep inside him he was flexing himself preparing himself, as desire flamed in him, to feel his master's cock inside him tearing to his depths.

As they kissed Lex gently stroked the crevice where the back strap of the thong had been pressing. He found the seat of longing and circled it. He brought his hand to Sandy's mouth and with it full of his wetness returned to his bottom and pressed a finger deep inside him making him gasp and buck and jump. He pulled out of him and pulled his legs apart and arched him up into a perfect parabola, his chest muscles straining against his skin, his arms folded behind his head.

His cock was his hunting spear, and he entered Sandy's forest with it and played up and down his anal canal, fast and slow and changing his rhythm and dancing inside him, giddy with the animal power of earth and sunshine. All of Sandy's beasts responded with a fury of disciplined movement and charged at him grabbing hold of him and with quick repetitions of in-out breaths pulled him in and danced around him. Arcs of excitement breaking across his body, throbbing like a wave rolling to its crest, flailing, Sandy assaulted Lex's face with wild kisses.

***

SANDY LIKED dressing in leather. He knew he was in good shape. He wasn't one of those queens who complain about something they know they have nothing to complain about, but are just fishing. Still, he thought, it could be better, better defined chest, get a little more tight contour in the ass.

He started working out, doing yoga and playing soccer. He liked the discipline of working out. It was his own special secret obedience training. He liked to dissolve in the heat of yoga and the awareness of his breath. He liked the masculine jazz of soccer. It was Brazilian dancing. He lost himself in everything.

It all added up to he looked great. He was pleased. Lex was very pleased and whispered in his ear, "You please me."

Sandy fell into a swoon and all his senses died, and in the hollow tunnel where something used to be, a tree began to grow, and his master's voice grew on the tree and he heard it leading to a stream from which he drank, stretched out beside it, his lips to the water.

**SANDY WAS** in leather -- pants, motorcycle jacket hanging open over bare, shaved chest and washboard abs, black leather band for a collar, boots, bareheaded. He was waiting at The Bat nursing a brandy at the bar, indifferent to all the concupiscent gazes directed at him.

Lex entered the room. The contrast was stark -- the one a leather slut to make men's mouths water; the other impeccably, elegantly attired in a gorgeous worsted suit and silken shirt, in shoes proud and supple of burnished leather, in such easy command of himself that it makes men daydream about worshipping him.

They approached each other and smiled. It was their conspiracy. They embraced and kissed and went over to the table that was waiting for them. Lex placed the flat of his palm under Sandy's jacket, cupping his hard breast, feeling his tight nipple. They knew they were being looked at.

A shy, young waiter with a high pompadour, wearing tight black trousers - they could see the discrete outline of his erection -- cummerbund, bow tie, a form fitting waistcoat and a tiny silver earring approached the table and bowed before inquiring if he might take the gentlemen's orders.

# End of the 2$^{nd}$ book

# ROYCE

## Gideon Elliot

# Royce

Arthur was known throughout the Village as Rex. For years he had taken men who fantasized about being slaves to places they had never before been. Some of them remained there and some returned, preferring where they had always been to the new territory they had just seen.

It was a ferocious nocturnal country he inhabited. To get there you dressed in black leather and you traveled by whips and chains. Nipple clamps, genital restraints, and devices for internal insertion were the passports.

For many who had dreamed of seeing the place, it was too scary when they got there and they booked a quicker return than they had intended, willingly paying the surcharge for leaving, losing something of themselves they had to abandon in order to get away. It was the ransom they paid to get themselves back, the phantom limb left in the trap.

A few knew at once that finally they were home, and never left, and never came back, and said they never had known themselves as well as now. Now they were the people they always had been and never had been able to be, and had always longed to meet.

You'd see them on the streets, those who remained, walking beside him, or behind him, sometimes on a chain leash, always collared, waiting for the snap of his fingers. By the look in their shaded eyes it was clear that they were far away, somewhere else.

I had known Royce before he became a bondage slave. I had been with him at Crazy Benny's the night Rex spotted him and put the eye on him. He had just passed his twenty-third birthday. It made my heart sink that he could be attracted to Rex. He knew it, too. He knew it grieved me. And Rex also knew it. He gave me one of his conspiratorial, devilish smiles. It was one cool embodiment of ironic cruelty. "Triumph," it said, and "fuck you." The more you suffered, the less you were able to resist the need to suffer, the more Rex enjoyed it. His face was handsome and in the rosy bar light, it appeared softer than it really was in daylight.

"Royce is a sweet kid," I said to him.

He took me by the scruff of the neck and kissed me, warmly, seductively, friendly, powerfully.

I lost my balance and gripped the bar stool to steady myself.

"I know he is," he said. "I like them sweet. Remember?"

"Show some mercy." I said.

"As I did for you?" he said.

"You call that mercy?"

"I let you go."

"I got away."

"Not very far."

He grinned.

I knew that Royce was as good as gone. I saw the way he was looking at us. He could see that Rex had power; anybody could. That turned him on. But I knew he had no idea what that power was and that his own cooperation could so greatly enhance it.

What Royce did not understand and would not believe me when I told him is that pain is as addictive as any pleasure. More so, in fact, because it is more powerful than pleasure! Pleasure ingratiates itself.

Pain asserts itself despite the resistance of the ego, which it must have the intensity to overpower. When pain goes to work, it takes over and makes sure you pay attention. It is the final authority. It will accept nothing less than mastery.

When Royce finally did believe me it only made him want it more.

Rex was interested in one thing, taking guys one step beyond where they wanted to go, and then one step beyond that.

I don't like melodrama. Love is a quiet thing. And I loved Royce. But the Royce I loved was hardly ever present, hardly ever the one who showed himself. So I loved the other one, the one who did, the one who was there, the one who got in the way, the only one you'd be likely to see, the one I compassionated for not really being Royce, for being his misrepresentation of himself.

"What are you hiding from?" I asked him that five years ago. We were in the showers in the basement of the gym we went to Wednesday evenings after classes.

"I'm not hiding from anything," he said, laughing, as he thrust his naked pelvis forward and soaped himself as he said it, as if illustrating its truth that very moment by that very gesture.

I could only smile and when I did, he stepped close to me and rubbed his soapy body against mine and blew on my neck and kissed me.

"I like that," I said, as he rubbed our hard soapy cocks together.

"I know," he said.

"I wish it could be like that always," I said.

"You've got to rinse yourself off sometime, captain," he said, as his semen gushed onto the soapy foam slicking my torso.

I knew he meant it, and I wished I had not said anything.

"How long were you with Rex?" Royce asked arching his left eyebrow as he brought the cup of sweet Turkish coffee to his lips.

"A few years," I said, showing my misgiving.

"Why do you say it that way?"

"Because it's nothing that makes me feel good about myself."

"You felt good about yourself then, when you were in it."

"I thought I did."

"You thought you did."

"I thought I did."

"But?

"But I didn't."

"But you thought you did."

"I was deceiving myself."

"But it didn't feel like it then?"

"Why are you so insistent?"

"Because I want to feel it, and I want you to say it's ok."

"It's not ok."

"But you did it."

"That's how I know. Sorry. I'd rather talk about -- or really, I'd rather not talk at all and just gaze into the depth of your eyes and feel your eyes doing the same thing, gazing into mine. Just like when we..."

But Royce frowned, and his eyes went flat and he made the face he makes when he's annoyed.

"What am I supposed to do?" I said.

His eyes widened. He pursed his lip and shook his head.

"I know what I'm going to do," he said.

\*\*\*

**REX SAW** himself in the bathroom mirror, naked muscular torso, arms raised, as he combed his hair and palmed what he combed with the other hand, shaping his thick light brown and trembling hair, unruly with life, into a perfectly lacquered turban, or helmet.

Bruno lay at his feet, like a dog at his feet, each nipple clamped and giving off a steady burning pain.

Rex kicked him.

"Tell me why I did that." His voice was charming, warm, inviting, but still, remote and scary.

"Because I deserve it, Sir."

Rex stopped his mouth, pressing the big toe of his bare foot against the boy's lips.

Eagerly, gratefully, Bruno kissed it. Then he wrapped his lips around it and gave himself to it in rapture.

Rex stooped and patted his head.

"Go," he said, kicking him away as he pulled his toe out of his mouth and swatting his behind. "Lay out my clothing for tonight."

It was not a leather night. Afterwards, who could tell? If something...

At forty-five Rex was in his prime, slender and muscled, handsome, roughly handsome. He could change the way he looked. His face was rugged and movie-star masculine, but sometimes it was pretty, and his blue eyes could change to violet.

Rex snapped his fingers. Bruno pulled out the plug that had sealed Him. He draped himself over the velvet covered horse Rex kept in his dressing room. He opened to his master's desire.

Hard like a rock and primed by a rush of anger that up-rushing from an inexhaustible pool of anger fueled his hardness, Rex strapped the boy. Silent tears rushed from Bruno's eyes. His body tensed. Rex entered him, tore his way into him, through him, destroyed him, and left him sobbing in ecstatic gratitude, alone, slumped over the velvet horse, listening to the silent sound of the air hissing and hearing a key turn in the lock.

Guys into all kinds of gear minced or strutted around in Crazy Benny's, gossamer fairies, underwear queens, engravings out of Tom O'Finland, dressed or undressed or partly, but no one came in a tuxedo.

"Where have you been?" Martin asked.

He was the nearest to an equal Rex had. It was awesome to watch Rex and him when they were together. Each riveted your attention and filled you with admiration. To see them being together was to glimpse a world of balanced power and of a mutual respect that neither of them found anyone else to be worthy of receiving.

It was then that Rex saw Royce, saw that he had seen him.

Royce had had a long night after a hard day. He had agreed to help his boss's partner take inventory at the antique store where he had worked, which closed after the robbery and his boss's murder. It had left Royce shaken but uninjured. And being in the store today had brought the events of only two weeks ago back.

He had had a few martinis after he got drilled in the eyes by Rex and before that we had smoked some special stuff in the alley.

He fell into my arms, touched my neck with his lips and said, "Comfort me."

I cradled Royce and kissed him with a father's heart all over his face as I rocked him back and forth.

"I don't know what I'll do," he said. "I want him so much."

I cradled and rocked him, and did not say "I tried to tell you."

"I'll be here. That's all I can say. I'm not sure what good it will do. I'll miss you."

"I won't go anywhere."

"If you go with Rex, you will."

"I'm afraid," he said. "And I'm excited."

"I know," I said. "It comes to be the same thing."

***

**REX SMILED** when Royce approached him, but it was at Martin, not at Royce. It was a smile for Martin, acknowledging something they both knew. His magnetism never gave him a moment's rest.

"Excuse me," Royce said, but Rex was slow to answer or even to acknowledge someone had addressed him. Royce added, as if the word were the stamp on the letter that would make it deliverable, "Sir."

Royce took my hand and looked into my eyes by the exit sign as he followed Rex out into the balmy Manhattan Street.

It was nearly four in the morning. You could stand in the center of the broad Ninth Avenue and look all the way up following the blazing trail of exploding amber lights along the rival sidewalks past midtown, and, if you turned, you could see the bifurcations at Fourteenth Street. The tough, old, queer, meat-market cruising ground, where hooks and trucks and the smell of carcasses came first, had become the illuminated landscape of dreams for men and women in sales, and design, and law, and advertising, for bodies drawn from fashion pages, for law clerks, and junior executives, and beginning stock brokers, and bond managers, bank tellers, and dentists, bit players, athletes, rockers, and fancy bohemians. Glittering with hopes, they were on the make.

Royce's eyes were glistering with a coating of tears, happy with a feverish intensity.

"It will be alright," he said, assuring me.

I embraced him and still held his hand as we parted.

I looked at his face, at the glowing complexion even at this hour, at the radiant flesh of his shapely arms and the upper part of his delicately sculpted chest. In my mind I saw his skin with bruises.

He let go my hand, turned sharply, walked quickly, caught up to Martin and Rex -- slowed down and took their pace when he was a few steps behind them.

"What you see in the symphonies of Beethoven," Martin said, drawing on his pipe and sipping at the cognac Rex had offered him, "is the desire of the individual to join with the mass in their mutual joyous declaration of common humanity, of merger and transcendence, whether in dancing, or marching, or in joint worship of the forces that live beyond the stars."

"But the twentieth century has shown pretty conclusively," Rex said, holding his cognac glass at the rim between thumb and first finger and perched on the arm of a leather settee, "how dangerous that is. By the end of the nineteen-thirties, the idea that the good of the individual was the proper end of collective endeavor had been defeated. Weimar gave way to Berlin, the Mensheviks to Stalin, republican Spain to Franco, the Popular Front to Vichy, workers' collectives to gulags. People have lost any belief in the wonder of the multitude, in the joyous communion of separated souls in one grand and overwhelming soul, which shines similarly in each heart and throbs simultaneously in each breast, and whose origin is in an unapproachably distant possibility."

"But they have not lost the yearning for it."

"No, they have not," Rex smiled. "Royce," he said, turning to the boy who had been sitting on the floor by the door to the study, listening wide-eyed to the strange conversation between these two men, "come here."

Royce stood and approached.

"Kneel," Rex said as Royce approached.

"Kneel?" Royce said.

"Kneel," Rex said in a voice more charged with impatience and command. There was no question but he must be immediately obeyed.

Royce obeyed, lowered himself to his knees and knew not further what to do.

"You see," Rex said, smiling, to Martin.

"He's very pretty," Martin said.

"Do you hear that?" Rex said, now addressing Royce.

"Yes, Sir," Royce said.

"What do you say?" Rex said, camping.

"Thank you, Sir," Royce said, not camping.

"You see," Rex repeated, looking at Martin.

"Do you know what it means to be one of my slaves?"

"No, Sir."

"But you want to become one of my slaves?"

"Not become, Sir."

"Not become?"

"I am your slave, already," Royce murmured, bowing his head. "My wish is that you accept me as your slave."

"Shall I accept him, Martin? What do you think?"

"May I examine him?"

"Certainly. Proceed."

"Stand up, Royce," he said nicely. "We are not going to hurt you now."

Royce stood.

"Bare your chest. Take off your shirt."

Royce pulled the black tank-top over his head, revealing a chest whose natural grace had been enhanced by determined and careful carving.

"You shave your chest," Royce, Rex said with delight.

"Yes, Sir," Royce said.

"Come here," Martin said. "I want to feel your nipples and see how hard your muscles are."

"Rex?" he added, checking for permission.

"Please," Rex responded.

This time Martin only gestured with a wave of his hand and Royce kneeled before him.

He took him by each nipple and began gently kneading them between his fingers, delighted to see how Royce shivered when he touched him. He began by squeezing and then dug the edges of his finger nails into firm nipple flesh until he led Royce to real, gasping pain. Royce struggled not to squirm and to hold himself tight and feel the authority of the pain coursing through him.

Rex stood up and went over to his mahogany desk, rummaged around the shallow top middle drawer and found two silver clamps.

"Here," he said to Martin. "Use these."

Martin let go of Royce's nipples and Rex clamped each, causing a sharp intake of breath. But rather than squirming, Royce tightened his body as if he were trying to become stone.

"Take off your jeans," Martin said.

Carved like a rock, his ass under the light microfiber of his black mini-boxers clenched him closed. Rex touched his forehead with his thumb. Royce felt a hollow rush up his center. His entrance had dilated with desire as his abs and pecs tightened.

"Congratulations," Martin said to Rex, and took him by the shoulder and brought him near. The two men shared a master's kiss together, each exercising his own and doing homage to the other's power. They pulled off their shirts and pressed their torsos together. Hard bodies pressed together, they pulled their trousers off, and then their briefs. Naked thigh to thigh they pressed their proud steely virilities together.

"You strip, too, Royce," Rex said. The boy complied and obeyed the summons to lie on his back and raise his legs. They broke into him.

"Please, Martin," Rex said. "You are my guest."

Martin was gentle. He appreciated that Rex was being hospitable, and he did not want to abuse his courtesy.

Rex, however, was not gentle. As was his way with his slaves, he asserted his mastery without concern for consequences. It was only then that he let down his guard and surrendered control, but only to his own passion.

Rex exploded inside Royce and set his nerves and muscles on fire.

I passed Royce on the street once, walking beside Rex. He was collared but not on a chain. He saw me and when he asked, Rex gave him permission to stop and say hello to me.

"You did it," I said, somehow knowing not to shake his hand or clasp him in a friend's embrace or kiss his cheek.

He bowed his head slightly, almost slightingly.

On the side of his neck, below his left ear, there was a small tattoo of orange flames.

"You look terrific," I said, recovering myself.

He did.

"I can't stay," he said as Rex watched us. Rex made no sign of greeting to me or even of acknowledging me, although I smiled at him and raised my right palm in a half salute.

That did not bother me. It had changed inside me. I was quits with him.

"Good luck, kid," I said.

Royce turned away from me. It seemed he gave me a secret wink as he did. At least, I thought so. But it was gone before I could be sure.

# End of the 3$^{rd}$ book

# The HOLLOW Man

## GIDEON ELLIOT

# The Hollow Man

It could not have been simpler. I was unhappy. I was on the verge of becoming isolated and bitter. I was trying to fight it by ignoring it. Not by denying it, just ignoring it. Not to give it scope. Not to grant it admission to the chambers of my heart. The thing to do was to crowd it out with other sensations.

In the past I would have run through phantom, endless, tortuous conversations in my mind with the shadow of the person who was not there until total depletion. After years of being torn apart and distraught every time a relationship crashed, however, I had finally developed a means of coping. I had learned to hypnotize myself. I stood in front of the bathroom mirror and stared into my own eyes with a penetrating vacancy.

Perhaps it was homeopathic, but I also used small doses of pain. Small doses of pain, properly administered, usually in the form of clips applied to my nipples while I did push-ups energized me. With that pain-induced energy I could push myself through several strenuous work-outs. The pain set me moving. That got me breathing. And I generally felt better afterwards, light, released. Not least, I felt a pride in myself which shattered relationships usually drained me of.

Pain! Strange! But yes, I who had always wept for pleasure, longed for it. I, who in my youth danced with lovers through the streets and sang as if we were back in a black and white Fred Astaire movie, now I was clamping my nipples and making them burn, and it made me yelp. But there it was.

December is a rotten time to be alone. But there I was. And I had two tickets for Henry the Fourth. We had gotten them months ago. But he was gone -- to Colorado. Skiing! The theater was not crowded, and I could not give the other ticket away. So the seat next to me was empty. It was convenient. I had some place to put my coat. There were quite a few empty seats in the theater. There were a lot of coats watching the show.

It had, without my knowing it, begun to snow. I was sitting in the theater, watching the drama of Henry IV unfold. Outside, the December streets, as the grizzled day tumbled into a phosphorescent night, right before Christmas, in mid-town Manhattan... the streets were preparing for me a fairy-tale luminosity. The Shakespearean imagination primed me, took me far into the realms of wish and wonder, made me entirely ready for it.

Strangely, too, I had even been prepared for the unexpected sight of the trembling boy that met me from across the street as I pushed open the brass and glass door leaving the theater lobby. He was shivering unmercifully in a moth-eaten overcoat. He crossed the street to try his luck in the not very thick, exiting crowd and, choosing me, approached with a plaintive and yet not wholly submissive request that I give him some change, spare change -- change I might spare, but not change I would give sparingly. If it were to be change, it would have to be a big change. That much was obvious from the depth of his gaze, from the depth of my heart. There was more life in that gaze than the moment might suggest.

"You need more than that," I said, looking at him with the scrupulous scrutiny you reserve for actors who approach you intimately without stepping across the proscenium of the stage and demand you meet them only in your thoughts, a scrutiny which you usually withhold from actual personages. From them, from actual people, this I knew, the necessity of caution and the dictates of survival demand you protect yourself. Once you let another person who actually exists gain a foothold in your consciousness, once you look with any kind of intent, to say nothing of allowing your sympathy to take hold, the dreadful chance is you may begin to discover you cannot live only for yourself, but must gather within that previously self-enclosed definition of yourself, somebody else. And then. And then.

Thus it was that as I looked at him, simultaneously I recoiled and then recoiled from that retraction and found myself propelled by an energy unusual to my schooled reluctance, my wise wariness. I invited the young man to go with me into the steakhouse at the corner of the street of theaters, amber in its lighting, advertising itself in gold lettering on a green panel that had an age-darkened warmth that, combined with the after-theater appetites of playgoers, beckoned invitingly those with money enough to enter.

"You are hungry as well as cold," I said rather than asked, told him as if to keep him from telling me.

"Yes," he said, allowing both wistfulness and a smile to rise from within him to inform the features of his face and present to me a beauty of physiognomy that I intuited before I had actually seen it and that would always frame him with a marvelous allure when he was illuminated by a sense of gratitude.

Had the restaurant been crowded, we would have been, undoubtedly, turned away, so unsavory was his appearance then and, in fact, inadmissible in that society of diners who shunned such a reproach to their self-satisfaction that his obvious need imposed upon it. But it was a quiet evening. Nearly everyone was home or almost, snuggling in the fantasy of family. So here in this inn we were allowed a reserved hospitality, comfortably hidden behind a full and fine and thickly ornamented Christmas tree.

Ill-clothed as he was, it was apparent immediately by the way he took his place at table and held the waiter's gaze despite that steward's studiously applied air of contempt in serving the table, that the young man was not ill-bred. Want of money had not been his birthright but something notoriously achieved. Begging was not his nature, but something to which he had been driven, or, it was a posture, more likely, a response to the disbalance of some forces -- internal or external, or a conflict of both? -- to assume which he had compelled himself.

\*\*\*

**"YOU WOULD** not take it amiss," I said, after we had eaten and had taken the last of our coffee, his, I saw, he had profusely sugared, "if I invited you back home with me where you might shower and change your clothes."

"Why should I take it amiss?" he asked with the lilt of a smile, which was perfectly attuned to the music of his voice, brightening his eyes.

"You should not," I said, and stood, and he did, too.

"But I have no other clothes," he said, "to change into."

"You can wear some of mine."

"Thanks," he said.

Outside, the snow had grown thick in its fall and we soon were in a cab, smelling like warm mint tea, being driven cautiously by a turbaned, bearded man down a nearly empty Ninth Avenue to Twentieth Street in Chelsea. Oddly (oddly?) the radio was tuned to a station playing Lester Young in a mellow mood doing I Can't Get Started with You.

"You don't have to do that," I said looking up from my book after he entered my study, clothed only in a towel and kneeling in front of the chair I sat in beside the fire blazing in the fireplace.

"I want to," he said, his gaze open and penetrating, astonishing to me that he was looking at me with an admiration I had thought would much more have befitted the way I ought to have looked at him. He was begging.

"Why does it make you sad?" he said.

"It does not make me sad," I said. And he did not pursue his intuition, although he was right. I could not have said why. To try to would have made me sadder.

"What are you reading?" he asked without rising from his knees in front of me, but rather now having slipped himself between my legs, which he had parted with a gentle assurance.

"The play I saw this afternoon, Henry the Fourth."

"'Once more unto the breach,'" he said.

"No," I said, smiling, "that's later. That's Henry the Fifth."

"But it's the same person," he answered.

"Yes, it is," I said. "Yes."

"We read it in college," he said, "but I dropped out before we finished the history cycle." He took the book from me and laid it on the side table and slipped his warm palm around the back of my neck and brought his fleshy lips to mine and breathed the sweet breath of youth and touched me with his silken tongue on mine.

"Is it alright I do that?'

"You don't have to," I said.

"You said that already," he said.

"I did. I know," I said. "But I don't want you to feel you have to, to reciprocate in any way."

"I know," he said. "But why do you think I would only want you from a sense of obligation?"

"You may if you like," I said, "sleep here tonight, if you have nowhere else to go but back into the street."

"And what about tomorrow night?" he asked with a mischievous smile.

"Tomorrow night, too."

"And the night after that?"

"And the night after that," I said. "And the whole winter if need be."

"If need be."

"If need be. I have an extra bedroom."

"You don't want me sleeping with you?"

"They are not my wishes I am consulting."

"What are your wishes?"

"I'm not sure where you are leading this."

"I did not think I was leading it anywhere," he said.

"It looks to me like you are," I said, touching his thick sandy-colored hair.

"I like when you do that," he said.

"I like to do it," I said.

"There," he said. "I like when you say what you like."

"Why are you doing this?" I said.

"Doing what?" he said.

"Weaving a spell."

"Am I weaving a spell?"

"Yes," I said, "yes, I think you are."

"Good," he said, and kissed me long and gently.

*** 

**WHAT WILL** you do today?" he asked in the morning after he had caressed my cheek and kissed me delicately.

"I don't know," I said.

"I would like to walk in Central Park," he said, "with you."

"Alright," I said.

"You have not asked me about myself," he said.

A sharp coldness, invigorating rather than congealing the blood, rose from the white-blanketed hills as we sauntered through the snow as if through fields of uncut grass in autumn.

"No," I said.

"Why not?" he asked. "Aren't you interested?"

"I'll listen to anything you want to tell me," I said, and kissed his forehead.

"Don't do me any favors," he said.

"I did not intend it to sound like a favor."

"What are you afraid of?" he said.

"Why do you think I'm afraid of something?"

"Don't answer a question with a question," he said, looking almost hurt.

"Alright," I said. "I'm not afraid of anything."

"I don't believe you," he said.

"Well, then, you seem to know better. You tell me what I'm afraid of."

He looked around and took my hand and drew me to him and looked tenderly into my eyes.

"You are afraid of falling in love with me."

"You're pretty sure of yourself," I said laughing.

"No," he said. "Don't laugh. I'm pretty sure of you."

At that moment, at least at that moment, if a physical response is any indication of love, he was right, for now I had begun to shiver, although my coat was not tattered as his had been yesterday.

"I think I better take you inside for a coffee," he said.

"I'd prefer brandy," I said.

"Let's go," he said.

We walked out of the park at 59th Street and over to Lexington Avenue to Russell's an old English style place with a mahogany bar, dark red leather booths and amber lighting.

"Why are you afraid to love me?" he said after we had touched glasses.

"Aren't you rushing things?" I said. "I met you yesterday."

"That's irrelevant."

"Irrelevant?" I said, almost condescending to his innocence.

He took my hand from across the table. We sat facing each other.

"Look," he said, "love defies time. When you met me, you entered a different dimension. You know that."

"And you, did you enter a different dimension when you met me?"

"No," he said.

"No?" I repeated.

"No," he explained. "I was there already, waiting for you."

"For me?"

"Why do you think I approached you yesterday when the street was full of people who had just come out of the theater?"

"Because I looked like a soft touch," I said laughing. "And because I was alone and probably more vulnerable."

"You are vulnerable, and you're afraid I'll hurt you, cause you pain."

I looked at him without saying anything, wondering just what he was doing, just where he was taking this.

"Perhaps you'd even like that, if I caused you pain. I might enjoy it myself. Make you beg."

"What are you doing?" I said.

"I don't know," he said. "Getting to know you?"

"You'd look really hot with pierced nipples and little diamond studs at the tips."

"What?" I said.

"You'd like it too. It would feel even better when I did this to you," he said and moved his lips away from mine where he had just been lavishing kisses on me, and like a frisky dog began biting my nipples with the tips of his teeth.

I shivered with immense pleasure and was lost in my own hardness.

"You see," he said, wrapping his palm around me and grinning.

"Are you the devil or what?" I said.

"I'm the devil that takes you to paradise."

"Or makes me into the kind of fool who mistakes hell for heaven!"

"Shut up and kiss me," he said, and when our mouths were pressed tenderly together and I was swimming in his warm moistness, he suddenly pinched my nipple and dug his nail into it. When I gasped and tried to pull away he pressed me tight to him by the palm behind my neck and would not let me go. He overloaded me with such sensations that I could not distinguish any more between pain and pleasure. My nipple felt ice cold and burning hot. I looked at him with amazement.

"Yes," he said.

"How did you know?" I said.

"I'm like that," he said.

As he broke me with kisses he pushed his long fingers inside me and played with me until I was grabbing for him every time he pulled out of me. He raised my legs over his shoulders and slowly entered me with his full hardness and filled my mouth with his saliva. I arched my back and rocked to pull him deeper down into me, never wanting to be doing anything but this.

At last he flooded me and I broke out in an overflow of spirit.

Afterwards, I was hollow without him still inside.

# End of the 4<sup>th</sup> book

# GIDEON ELLIOT

# LUCAS

# Lucas

I adore him. He is rugged, cultured, handsome, well-wrought, powerful. I worship him. I melt when I think of him. I throw myself at his feet. I caress his thighs. I lick his boots. I tremble when I think of him.

He is severe in his demands and swift in administering discipline for infractions or failures. But once you understand what he requires, once you have overcome the frailties in yourself, the weaknesses and inhibitions that might hinder your ability to serve and submit, it becomes clear that there are few men who are his equal.

He is a man who has the ability to fold you entirely into himself, to protect you from everything, including yourself, and to give you a sense of certainty, clarity, and, yes, of bliss. Devotion to him seems less like a duty than a privilege. To be disciplined by him turns punishment into a reward.

He had found me at a time when I was consuming myself with rage. Everything, everything made me angry. Encounters with other people always ended in an argument and, more often than not, in a fit of misdirected venom erupting from within me, like lava from a volcano supposed to be inactive but with a hidden molten core.

I shook and my blood quivered for hours after such explosions.

\*\*\*

**I WAS** sipping espresso outside a cafe in the rue Vieille du Temple, unable to stop my mind from grinding on about regrets and resentments that clung to me like barnacles that no amount of scraping could loosen. I was looking at the crowd flowing past, lots of tourists, knobby of knee, flabby of, well just flabby, wearing again at forty, fifty, and sixty the same kind of clothes they wore at four, five, and six, dressed in tasteless colors like graceless children in hideous summer vestments. But every now and then someone would go by who belonged in another world. I was consumed by frustration and longing.

"God damn it," I cried out in English to the big-bellied American in Bermuda shorts and a rust colored football jersey who banged the metal leg of a chair sharply into my heel as he pulled the chair back to lower his bulk into it. "Can't you fucking look at what you're doing?"

"Sorry, bud," he said with a stupid smile. "Guess you oughtta be careful where you put your feet."

"I'll put my feet up your ass," I said, but a man I had not seen prevented me from going further. He calmed the offended American and defused the encounter. He took hold of another chair, one alongside mine. He smiled at the American, and with a shrug, he raised the palm of his free hand and wordlessly told him to drop it.

Shaking his head the American said, "They warned me about France," but he retreated and sat with his back to us secure among his friends at his own table.

The handsome stranger sat down beside me.

"He's not worth it," he said in French.

"I know that," I answered.

"Then why do you waste yourself on him?" he asked. "Do you want to get beaten up?"

"I don't know," I said as I stared at him dazzled and in awe. Then bridging my forehead with thumb and three fingers, I looked at the cobblestones on the road and bitterly shook my head.

It was not what I wanted to do. I wanted to charm and fascinate and draw him to me. But all I could do was withdraw. I hated myself.

"Look," he said.

"Yes," I said.

"And listen."

"I am, "I said.

"You're too loose," he said. "You've got energy and grit, but no discipline."

He was speaking in English now.

"You are blown here and there and anywhere by every wind. You need to be anchored."

"Anchored?" I repeated.

"Anchored," he said.

"You mean kept in one spot with a chain and a heavy weight?" I asked making a joke.

"When necessary, yes," he said, with complete seriousness, not joking.

"But..."

"Don't respond to something I tell you by saying 'but,'" he said quietly.

Obviously, I did not have to stay sitting next to him. I'd put a two euro coin on the round marble top table already, and I was as free as I would ever be to get up and leave. But I did not. I stayed seated and I kept looking at him. He was extraordinarily handsome and he was frightening. That was evident immediately.

Every angel is terrible. There was something terrible about him in the absolute power to compel that nature had vested in him and that he wore effortlessly. We were bound to each other from the bottom of our being. I was bound to him whether or not he was bound to me. That's what was frightening. He was something I knew I could not avoid. It was danger, and this time I couldn't get away from it. I was in his grip before I knew his name.

He took hold of me gently, cupping his palm around the back of my neck. I turned to face him, and as I did he brought his lips to mine and the culmination of my gesture became his kiss.

That he wanted me gave me the sense that I had worth. I gave myself up to him.

\*\*\*

**RUE VIEILLE DU TEMPLE** branches off on the right as you are walking towards rue de Bretagne into rue des Rosiers. Not far from that corner stands a small, three story eighteenth-century house.

His apartment had high ceilings, marble chimneys, ornate molding, and parquet floors. It took up the entire top floor. In the front the windows gave out onto the street and offered a panorama of rooftops and sky. In the rear, they gave onto a splendid garden.

"And if you don't pass your exams?" Lucas said, picking up the thread of our conversation as he poured out some brandy for us.

"The money stops, I go back to New York, and work in my father's costume jewelry factory," I said. "And, I'm afraid that's what's going to happen," I added. "I am not prepared."

"Not prepared."

"For the exams."

"And not for going back either."

"For sure."

"You don't want to do that, to go back to New York and work in your father's factory?"

"No," I said, "I don't."

"You like to get beaten up." He raised his glass as he spoke, as if toasting and then put it to his lips.

I looked at him in confusion. "You said that already," I said.

"Yes," he said and nodded for me to drink, too. The brandy burned my insides.

"How did you allow it to happen?" he said. I was silent. "What happened?" Lucas persisted. "About school?"

"I don't know," I said. "I guess I fucked up."

"You fuck up a lot."

"Yeah," I admitted.

\*\*\*

**"TAKE YOUR** clothes off," he said.

I was standing by the window looking into the street.

"Take off your clothes." He spoke with a tone of command in his voice that excited me. It was impossible to disobey. I unbuttoned my shirt, pulled it off, loosened my belt, undid my shoe laces and stripped down to my black boxer briefs. I was tight.

"Leave those on. I like the way you look in them."

I blazed with pleasure and shame. "Yes, Sir," I said, intending a funny flash of mockery to keep my balance, but the words came out differently.

"Bring me that silver box from above the fire place," he said, gesturing to an elegantly wrought art nouveau object.

"Yes, Sir," I said, this time with no thought of making a joke.

\*\*\*

**HE HELD** my arms over my head in one hand at the wrists while he tongued and bit my nipples. I melted. I dissolved. I was powerless. He raised himself and kissed me on the mouth, commanding entrance by the force of his tongue, as he continued to hold me by the wrists. With the other hand he probed me and entered deeply into me with his fingers.

He raised my legs over his shoulders and I embraced him with them. He stretched his length above me and penetrated beyond the ring of pain into the crystalline globes of ego-destroying pleasure. I decomposed into shimmering circles of blue and gold cosmic dust.

He rang inside me like a city of bells, like all of Amsterdam, like a countryside full of gonging, clanging, tolling steeple bells banging out a head-spinning cacophony of joyful tintinnabulation.

\*\*\*

**THE GARE MONTPARNASSE** was overcrowded with throngs of soccer fans. They were all dressed alike, exactly alike, in red jerseys. They hooted, clapped, banged noisemakers, and chanted cheers.

They made waves of sound swell and vibrate inside the volume of their voices. They gave energy an aspect of matter. It took up space in the terminal.

Lucas and I were there because we were going to Chartres to see the great cathedral. I was afraid they would not let me in because of how I was dressed. I would not have dared say that to Lucas. It would have possibly suggested that I did not trust his authority or that there was a hesitation in my obedience.

When I began to live with Lucas, he kept me naked. When I had to be clothed, when we were going out or a stranger was in the house, I was only allowed to wear torn clothing. When we were by ourselves and when Lucas wished, I sometimes wore a leather thong. The thin strap that connected the front pouch to the waist band continually stimulated the hole though which Lucas entered me.

I had been with him for half a year and had responded well to his training. Why would I not have? I had messed everything else up. He was the center of all order. I had been aimless. He transcended purpose. He was a powerfully commanding man. From the start, I worshipped him. I loved him to my extinction. Submitting to him, being controlled by him, obeying him all excited me.

He had not often chained me, and he had seldom had to punish me. Sometimes he punished me not for a fault, but simply because it was part of the nature of things that he punish me. When I did vex him, his vexation was more painful to me than the punishments he administered and the penalties he imposed.

To go without the sweetness in his eyes was worse that standing like a statue, naked in an alcove, my hands behind my neck, tiny clamps on my nipples and a tight ring snug at the base of my cock. When he invited visitors at such times, they fingered me as they had never been allowed to when they looked at Michelangelo's David or Dying Captive in a museum.

For the trip to Chartres, I had on jeans that were ripped at the knees over a leather jock, an olive colored t-shirt with a rip exposing my right nipple, Pakistani water buffalo sandals, and a collarless, zip-up, brown, leather jacket, unzipped.

Lucas wore all black, boots, leather slacks, a long sleeve, ribbed cotton pullover and a cotton velvet jacket, black and tapered at the waist.

With a firm arm round my shoulders he guided me through the crowd to our track. He composted our tickets and we sat on the upper deck as the train plowed out of Paris into the green and brown countryside, past Versailles, on to Chartres.

Not far from the railroad station, stands the great cathedral with two spires which do not match rising above its Gothic front. The massive stones soar above the earth and become, the higher they rise, the more delicately wrought, until stone is worked more finely than filigree or damask lace.

A young man sat on one of the long marble steps leading up to the church porch. He was staring at us as we approached. He was beautiful, perhaps not yet twenty, and glowed with freshness. His skin gave off light, like a bowl of early summer fruit. He had thick dark hair, dark perfectly arched eyebrows, high cheekbones and full lips. He needed a shave.

Lucas made a point of walking up the church steps directly in a path leading to him, and when we were near him, sidestepped just enough to pass him but near enough to rub his head with the friendliness with which you would pat a dog you passed.

"Hey," the young man said in English, his composure ruffled as well as his hair.

"Hey, yourself, Angel," Lucas answered him with a big grin. "You all by yourself?"

"Yeah."

"Alone?" The young man shrugged.

"That's not the way it ought to be," Lucas said. "Where you staying?"

"Camp out, ride the train."

"What's next?"

"Hitchin' to Paris."

"And?"

"See what's there."

"Were there. Come with us. Nick won't mind," he said, pointing to me with his thumb. "We're going back after we've seen the cathedral. Been inside?"

"Not yet."

"Come in with us," Lucas said, stretching out his hand for the boy to grasp and stand himself up.

No one stopped me from entering, dressed as I was. We walked through the cavernous, vaulted, stone cathedral, glowing golden from the candles lit throughout and reverberating with the deep blue and luminous red that form grand patterns on stained glass.

Lucas put his arm round the boy, guiding his attention to a detail of stone filigree crowning the marvelously wrought semi-circular stone wall in the ambulatory behind the altar. He whispered with warm breath in his ear and it spilled onto the enthralled boy's neck with such heat that he was not sure the man was not kissing him on the side of his neck.

Afterwards, as the sun set, we sat in the square outside the cathedral, still lost in admiration and drinking coffee. The boy was coming home with us. He was awestruck by Lucas, more by Lucas than by Chartres, and he was trying to hide it. But he was blissed out: one hand fingering his small coffee cup, the other invaginated in Lucas's palm.

On the train back to Paris he slept sprawled out on the seats across from me. Lucas from his seat at the window turned to look at me and make sure that I was aware that he had seen me gazing at the beauty stretched out in front of me.

"Say thank you," he said.

"Thank you," I said.

***

**LUCAS ESTABLISHED** a household for the three of us, a menage a trois.

The boy and I were both in need. I had not gotten through the semester at the Sorbonne, and all bets were off for me ever having anything near the life I wanted to have if I went back to the States to work for my father. They'd get me married somehow to a lovely young woman I would grow old with and make her miserable, just as she would be my torment. Lucas allowed me to stay in France by inviting me to stay with him.

The boy Lucas called Angel had left America during the last year of high school. He did not want to register with the military even if there wasn't a draft. The whole idea of soldiers or even universities gave him the creeps. He wanted to be on the move and he got himself to Europe. He was fortunate his Italian mother got him put on her passport when he was born. He could travel pretty easily now because he had both an American and a European Union passport. He could stay put too, wherever he wanted to.

Lucas told him to stay.

"There's nothing in this arrangement that you need to feel threatens you," he said to me, as he sat with Angel in a small room off a long drawing room. I looked quizzical. "Come here."

I stood up and walked over to him. He stood, too, and approached me. He took me in his arms and pressed his hard body against mine and gave me a kiss that took hold of something essential, of my very identity, and made it his.

Then he moved me aside. With the slightest gesture, slightly raising his index finger, he indicated that I remain where he set me and quietly attend.

"Angel," he said.

If I were going to care about exclusivity, I was going to have a lot of suffering and pain to endure. But I trusted Lucas, and a current of excitement shot through me.

Lucas directed us to embrace each other. I felt the strength of his body pressing min. It made me feel the strength of my own body. I felt desire for him as strong as the desire that Lucas felt. I knew that and realized how great a pleasure Lucas derived from possessing him and spending himself on him. It thrilled me. But he was allowing me to experience what I was not going to have again.

By the magnetics of our own being Angel and I were drawn to each other and our mouths pulled us into a kiss. Lucas let us go to its depths. Then he stopped us.

"You've tasted the sweet fruit that after this is forbidden to you."

So it was. We looked at each other always with hot eyes, bound together, longing to clasp, and never touched.

On a snow-heavy evening Lucas posed me in an alcove in his bedroom as Michelangelo's 'Dying Captive' with my head thrown backwards in an agonized and ecstatic swoon. I stood in the alcove like a decoration in a Cocteau movie. And that was the last notice taken of me that night although everything was performed in front of me, within my sight.

Lucas beheld the boy and powerful desire rushed through him and grasping appetite propelled him. He took command with his gaze. He brought the boy close to him and claimed him with a binding kiss.

"You belong to me."

"I knew I was the moment I saw you."

Lucas bit him with a kiss and held him in the palm of his hand slowly massaging him at the fork of his body. He took him in his orbit and held him with his gaze as he very slowly moved in and out of him, turning him crazy with the need to be penetrated.

Watching them, I trembled like a quivering string. I overflowed my banks. I came without touching myself, still, keeping the statuary pose.

# End of the 5<sup>th</sup> book

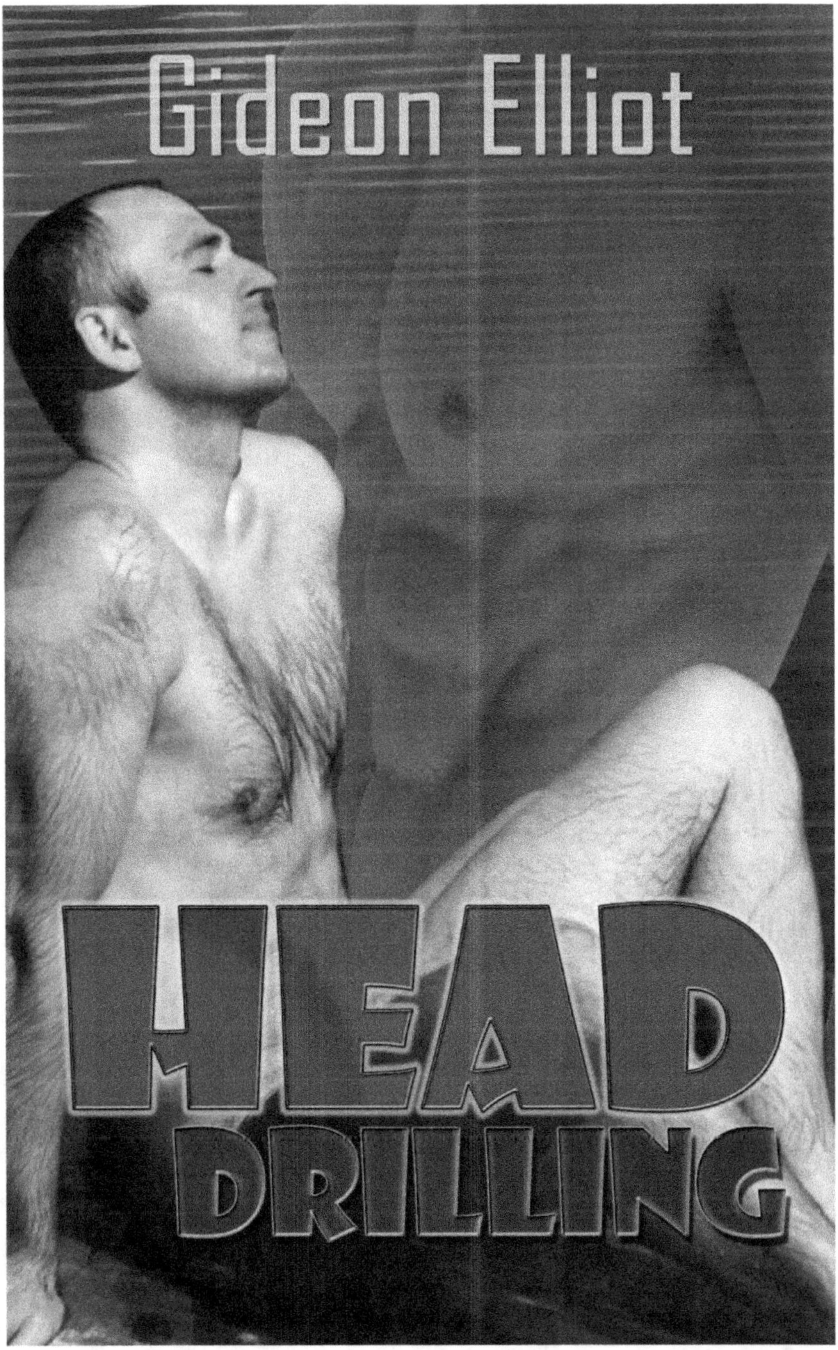
Gideon Elliot
HEAD
DRILLING

# Head Drilling

"Where have you been?" he asked quietly, tonelessly as I pushed the door to the apartment open as slowly as possible in order not to make noise.

You could hear when I answered that my voice was stuck way at the back of my throat. "Walking around. Went for coffee."

"Did you meet anyone?"

I couldn't lie if I tried. He always knew. "Yes," I answered, pulling my sweatshirt over my head.

"And?"

"And," I shrugged guiltily, standing there in my ripped-at-the-nipple t-shirt.

"Pussy itch got so bad, you couldn't wait."

"Yes, sir," I said with my eyes cast down.

"Like every other whore I've ever known."

"I'm sorry, sir."

"You like being a pathetic slut."

"I can't help it, sir."

"But I can," he said, pinching my exposed nipple with not half the force I knew he could apply.

"Thank you, sir," I said, dreading what lay in store for me.

"A slut!" he said laughing and shaking his head and letting go my nipple.

The rest of the day passed in an ominous quietude. I had laundry to do, and dinner to prepare, and my daily work-out in the basement gym. He was friendly. For me that made the tension unbearable. I knew he had not finished with me. I couldn't relax knowing the storm wasn't over. It hadn't even begun. But I could tell, balmy as it might be, the weather was heading over in that direction. There was going to be an explosion. I did not know when or how it was going to happen. But I knew anything could set it off.

He went out around three without telling me, and I wasn't sure when he'd be back. But I still couldn't relax because he might return at any minute. Fortunately I had begun a Boeuf Bourguignon the night before, right before I went out. So I drained off the marinade and set to cooking the stew. It smelled delicious by the time he returned. I'd set the table in an alcove off the living room by the French windows, and got candles and flowers. I showered after my work-out and gave myself an enema. I was wearing a sparklingly white sleeveless athletic shirt that fit me like a glove, a pair of brown leather trousers that I knew he liked and a pair of calf-hugging brown boots that gave a good thrust to my hips.

"Tonight you want to be a high-class whore, right? Not like yesterday."

I smiled and said, camping, "If you'll have me," but I felt my efforts to please him belittled.

"We'll see," he said, and walked over to the liquor table and took some brandy. He didn't offer me any, but then, after he had re-corked the bottle, as if a second thought, he said, "Oh, did you want any?"

"No thank you," I said.

"You're gonna need it," he said with a wink. "But now it's too late. Too bad."

"Shall we have dinner, sir?" I asked.

"I was waiting for you," he said.

\*\*\*

**"HOW MANY** bay leaves did you put in the marinade?" he asked holding a cube of beef and a sliver of mushroom under his nose before he tasted it.

"Three," I said nervously.

"No you didn't," he said. "You only put in two."

"I used three, really."

He grimaced at being contradicted, took a bite of the beef, and chewed with deliberation. "Two," he said.

I knew even before he said it that he did not believe me and there was no way I could convince him, even though I was there and he wasn't. Then I began to doubt myself and worry if I could really trust my own memory, and maybe....

"But this is all so trivial," I thought to myself. "He's fighting with me over a fucking bay leaf."

"Don't sit there sulking in silence," he said, but I could not say anything.

"I bet you're a pretty chatty whore when you're out on the street picking up some sweaty het."

I looked down at my plate and didn't say anything.

"Well," he insisted.

"Sometimes we talk; sometimes, not much."

"Just quietly get down to business."

I try to look at him unagressively. I want to get through this without saying anything wrong, with as little bloodshed as possible.

What if I have feelings that I shouldn't have? It got twisted when I try to think about it. That's what this always comes down to. That's the question that haunts me. What was wrong with cruising or making it with a guy who turned me on as long as we protect ourselves? I didn't have sex for money. I wasn't a whore. But I couldn't say that to him.

The words just wouldn't come: the thoughts would disappear before they were formulated. I couldn't argue with him. And if I could, he would not accept it. He wouldn't believe me.

It would have been heaven had he relented. There is such beauty and warmth in his face when he is free of the demons that plague him and he smiles at me as if he were giving himself to me.

I daren't, of course, say such a thing to him. He reprimands me saying it is not because he is driven by demons but because I make him angry that he is as he is, and then he says I hear it as a reprimand whenever he tries to tell me something.

I cleared the table as he sat with a cigar and another brandy. I usually don't like tobacco smoke, but this was almost pleasant, sweet and chocolate.

"The cigar smoke smells particularly good this evening," I said.

"You can open the kitchen window if it bothers you," he said as if I had complained about it.

"No, I like it. I mean it," I said.

He let out a long cloud of smoke slowly, and said, "Whatever."

One more time, he cut me off in an attempt to draw us into an affectionate conversation.

When I had finished cleaning up, I sat down across from him on a round leather hassock. I wanted to say something, but my mind was blank. I knew whatever I said, however well-intentioned would get twisted into something he would pick at. A spray of icy water trickled here and there inside me. I sat quietly, waiting for him to begin. I was ready to go through whatever he was going to put me through. I just wanted to get it over with, get it out of the way. I was equally prepared for affection or aggression.

"What would you do?" he began, as if he were posing a philosophical problem for class discussion, slowly inhaling his cigar and sipping his brandy.

"Sir?" I said.

"Don't sir me. I asked you what you would do," he said, patiently but on the verge of losing patience.

"Regarding what?" I asked, afraid I knew where he was going.

"Regarding whaattt?" he exploded. "You know perfectly well regarding what."

I sat there without speaking.

Finally I said, "Sir, I can't tell you anything if I don't exactly know what you're talking about."

"I arrive at one-thirty in the morning," he said with an anger that was worse because he was controlling it, "from the airport, in a taxi, expecting a warm greeting, someone at home, a midnight snack. But it's too much. You don't benefit from my trip to California? It's not your contract I negotiated?"

I was silent.

"Well," he said, glaring at me.

"It's my contract," I said.

"Damn right," he said, "and a damned good one, too."

"Thank you," I said. I wanted to add, "You know the money I make goes to you." But I thought better of it and swallowed the words in silence. All the same, I knew that he knew that I was thinking that.

"So what would you do?" he came back to the question I hoped he would let go of.

I was silent and looked down.

"The paddle?" I said, knowing, sooner or later, I'd have to. So just get it over with.

"Perhaps," he said, for starters. "You'd like that. A little humiliation. Isn't that what you like? Isn't that why you dress like a whore?"

He was getting furious as he spoke, and before he had finished he had slapped my left cheek so hard that I staggered backwards and nearly stumbled into a table lamp. Trying to avoid knocking into it, I fell. He was above me with a riding crop he'd taken from above fireplace.

I was still in my leather trousers. They protected me from the slap on the thigh being anything more than the rich sound of leather slapping against leather.

"You pig," he said shaking his head in quiet fury.

The nights had become chilly; the days were still warm. He opened wide both French windows and cold gusts blew chill into the room.

"Strip," he commanded.

***

**HE WAS** right. I do have an itch pussy. My ass-cunt was throbbing with desire for his cock. But I knew I'd have to wait for that, wait until he'd tortured and abused me, made me so raw that when he finally took me I would be screaming in pain for him to stop, on the edge of exploding but also unable to.

He was in no rush, and I was even afraid that he would not even bother disciplining me and just leave me to cool off standing in the slave position, stripped to a jock, in a chilly room all by myself.

"That's the one," he said returning, I didn't know how much later, with two other men, muscled and with a distinct mark of cruelty on their faces.

"He had everything, wealth, a loving wife, a shot at being a partner in a prestigious law firm, but hc fucked it up because he's got a very itchy pussy. It doesn't let him concentrate on much of anything for very long except how fucking horny he is and how much he wants some hard cock up his ass."

I cringed inwardly -- I did not dare show any outward response – when I heard him, especially because it was true.

One of the men approached me, opened my mouth and touched the aback of my tongue with his forefinger. I gagged.

"Good," he said. "Good gag reflex. Very important in a cocksucker. You are a cocksucker, aren't you?" he said with disdain, addressing me for the first time.

"Yes, sir," I said.

"Try mine," he said.

"Now, sir?"

"Right now, cunt," he said, pointing for me to kneel. I obeyed.

"Cunt," he repeated under his breath.

He wrenched me by the hair. "I felt teeth," he said.

## THE END

Here is a sample from another story you may enjoy:

5-BOOK BOX SET
Blue
Identity
Gay Erotic Romance
GIDEON ELLIOT

There was nothing more I could do. He was gone and I knew there was no way I could bring him back. Perhaps that was a good thing. Perhaps it wasn't.

What I could do was take a shower, scrub myself down, shave, get dressed, go out and get a haircut, buy some new clothes, work out at the gym, go for a drink at Benny's, stop in at the new sushi place on Barrow Street, get home around midnight, get stoned, listen to Jauchtzet Gott in Allen Landen, the Schwarzkopf recording, jerk off, and get some sleep. Tomorrow morning I'd go into work.

It would keep me busy. It would keep me going. And that's really all that mattered after all.

* * *

Ellen was waiting for me on the doorstep when I got home.

"You look better than I expected," she said.

"What did you expect?"

"A wreck," she said.

"Sorry to disappoint you," I said.

"I'm not disappointed," she said. "I'm glad. Anybody after almost ten years..."

"What are you doing?" I said, quietly.

"What do you mean?"

"You know perfectly well what I mean."

It never failed. She was getting me angry. The last thing I needed. It was a trick of hers. But I caught myself in time.

"I don't want to do this, Ellen," I said with no affect.

"You don't want to do what?" she said.

She was baiting the hook. She'd use any response as a way into a fight. Fighting was foreplay for her. I wasn't having it, and I wasn't going to explain. Even that was a way of involving me. I wasn't even going to explain why I wasn't going to explain.

"Good night, Ellen," I said unlocking the door to the building.

"You don't know what's good for you," she said, on the verge of crying.

It wasn't going to work.

"Perhaps," I said. "But I'll deal with it. Good night." I let myself in and disappeared behind the door, closing it gently behind me, leaving her there.

Actually, I felt better than I thought I would.


If you enjoyed this sample then look for **Blue Identity**.

**Also by this Author**

# About the Author

Gideon Elliot was born in 1981 in Wichita, Kansas.

He grew up in San Francisco and spends the greater part of the year, now, on one of the Cyclades Islands in Greece where he runs a jazz café, paints, writes poetry, and swims.

He has a small apartment in Greenwich Village, where he stays from the middle of November to the end of April and, during those months, manages an erotic men's clothing shop. He began writing erotic fiction at the age of fifteen.

**You may also like the books by these authors:**

# SUMMER
# AWAKENING

*Gay Romance*

## DICK PARKER

The summer after I graduated from high school was one that I'll never forget. I was eighteen, horny twenty-four seven and pretty sure I was gay. I'd never really had an experience that made me sure but I'd seen and done enough to know I liked looking at naked boys a lot more than I liked looking at naked girls.

Then my life changed. I met Aaron Strand.

\*\*\*

I lived in a new housing tract outside of Green Bay. My parents both worked at the hospital, my dad was a doctor and my mom an administrator. They worked a lot of hours and I had a lot of time home alone. I didn't get a summer job because I was going to start college in the fall and thought I'd just fuck around all summer and have some fun.

I'm pretty much what you'd call a typical eighteen-year old. I'm six-foot one and weigh in at about a buck forty. My dad calls the way I wear my hair, "Just got up". It's brown but gets pretty light in the summer. I have blue eyes and while I'm not a muscle man I'm okay. I was a late bloomer. I grew four inches during the previous summer and I'm smooth as a baby except for some armpit hair and my bush. My legs are smooth but I'm getting some hair on my lower legs.

I've seen a few dicks in the showers at school and I think I'm pretty much average. I've only seen a few guys with boners, and most of them were in a magazine a buddy showed me. It was a porn magazine and there were guys fucking girls. I looked at the guy's dicks. The pussy didn't turn me on.

Of course my buddy was looking at the pussy and we both ended up getting hard. We laughed and made fun of each other's bulge and he suggested we jack off together. Well I was nervous as hell. I didn't know if my dick was big or small and didn't want him to pull out a big fucking sausage and make me look like a midget, but I agreed.

We both were blushing as we pulled our pants down. His dick was uncut. I'd only seen a few like that. It popped up out of his shorts and hit his belly. I would have guessed it about six inches and average thickness. Mine was the same size but I'm cut. Mine sticks straight out. He skinned back the foreskin and his looked like mine. I really liked the look of it and really wanted to touch it, but I was too chicken. We lay back on the end of his bed and began jacking off. We'd look over at each other and laugh and soon we both came. His cum shot up on his nipple. I wanted to touch his cum and taste it but again I was too damn chicken. We wiped off and that was it. I went home and jacked off three more times that day. My dick got all sore and chafed so I had to take a day off from jacking it.

My dick, while not huge is between five and six inches and pretty thick. Mine was actually thicker than my buddy's. From that day on I had the image of his hard dick in my mind when I jacked off, so I began to think that I was probably gay.

\*\*\*

Our house was the ninth in a line of sixteen houses that all looked the same. They were typical for a sub-division where a builder started on one end of a street and built a bunch of identical houses. The only difference was the color of the roof and siding.

The house next to us had been vacant for about three months. The people who lived there had relocated to the south and I was pretty interested when a moving van backed up in their driveway. I sat on our front porch and watched as the men began opening the van up. A car drove up and a man and a woman got out.

They began telling the moving men where things went. They were both about the same age as my parents, forty, and they were very blond and good-looking. I heard them talking and knew they were from somewhere else because they had an accent. Being kind of nosey I walked across the lawn.

"Hello, I'm Nolan Redmond," I said. "I live next door."

Up close they were really handsome people. They had very blond hair and deep blue eyes. They both smiled and shook hands with me.

If you enjoyed this sample then look for **Summer Awakening**.

# BAREBACK
# ON BOARD

## DEXTER CHASE

Twenty-four hours to go and the ship would be docking in Plymouth. The atmosphere on board was electric. Two thirds of the crew had been away for thirteen months so they were champing at the bit to get back to their loved ones. It should have only been eight months but thanks to Muslim fanatics they had remained in the Gulf to support the legitimate government as allies.

Peter de Salis was one of the other third. He had been on board for a few months learning his way around his department. He would remain in the ship for the long refit and work up with the new crew before the ship returned to South East Asia and he would move on to a new appointment.

Peter was a communications officer and stood a lot of mickey taking. Com officers had hyphenated names, or at least that appeared to be the case so he was always being told he was in the wrong branch. He was a lieutenant, head of his department at only 24 years old. He had been commissioned straight from school and therefore received his university education on the pay of a sub-lieutenant. He graduated at 21 with a first class degree, had been promoted to lieutenant straightaway, and became a communicator.

The captain believed that all of his officers should be able to run the ship if needs be, so at sea while making passage, officers like Peter would have to do a stint as second officer of the watch. A waste of time during the night watches, and that was why Peter, at two in the morning had been allowed to go down to his office to collect some paperwork he needed to do before the ship docked. He opened the door to the operations room and was about to turn on the lights when he saw a beam of light coming from the bottom of the door leading into his office. He brought out his cell phone, prepared to take some quick pictures if there was mischief afoot. No one should be in his office without his permission, and certainly not at two in the morning.

Peter opened the door and immediately took about a dozen pictures as he moved into the office and walked round the four young men that were there. They didn't move. They just looked at Peter with shocked expressions on their faces. Not surprising really. All four were naked. Two of them had their cocks up the arses of the other two.

"Watkins', I think you can remove your cocks from the Arnolds."

They did. Peter went round his desk and sat down.

"Do any of you know what punishment will be handed out at your Court Martials when these pictures are displayed?"

All four of them nodded their heads and looked terrified.

"I believe it is four years in a military prison followed by a dishonorable discharge. Let me see, you four are eighteen and nineteen so at 22 and 23 you will become civilians again after four years in prison. I imagine that will be a recipe to confirm the ruination of your lives. Would you agree with me?"

They nodded their heads more.

Adam Arnold was the baby of the four with regards to maturity and it showed. Tears were running down his cheeks. Four years seemed like an eternity to him.

Peter looked along the line of the four. These were the four communications ratings that had joined the ship with him on the same terms: remain with the ship during refit, go to sea for the shakedown with the new crew, and then be off for a new appointment. Under normal circumstance they could all have been leading ratings by the time of their new appointments. He saw Adam's tears and wanted to wipe them away then hug the boy and tell him everything would be alright.

"Charlie, how could you be so careless? Why didn't you lock the door?"

Charlie looked sick, "Didn't think anyone would be around at this time of night, Sir."

Peter shook his head. "Well, you are bloody fools, all four of you. Stand at ease."

The four had been standing rigidly at attention until this point. Peter had scoped them out while he spoke to them and realized they were probably the most stunning young men on the ship. He was as hard as he had ever been looking at them. Fortunately, he was wearing his uniform jacket which would hide the bulge in his groin if he stood up.

If you enjoyed this sample then look for **Bareback On Board**.

# Turn Me Gay

## Chris Johns

# 5 Gay Stories in 1

CHRIS JOHNS' GAY COMPILATION, VOL. 6

This **Turn Me Gay** collection is running wild with the **most explicit Gay Erotica** possible, with pulsating tales of forbidden gay lust. If you love sexy men fulfilling their every gay sex fantasy, reaching a shuddering climax that will leap off the page and straight into your hot zones, then this is for you!

**5 Gay Erotic Stories in One Book:**
1. The Isle of Sexual Survival
2. The Rich Boy's Affair
3. Taboo Education
4. Summer Heat
5. Take it off

*For Mature Audiences Only(18+)

If you enjoyed this sample then look for <u>Turn Me Gay</u>.

# BAD SHERIFF

## REDNECK SPEED TRAP

GAY HARDCORE

ANGUS MACGREGOR

Arlo Givens took a long drink of coffee and slid down further into the front seat of his patrol truck. He turned the radio down to a lower volume than he kept it normally. He closed his eyes and held the radar gun lazily in his left hand. He was backed into one of his favorite spots, behind a large billboard promising homemade fried pies at Ethel's Kitchen. From here, he could see all the way east and west on Hwy 69 that ran through the backwater town of Lone Pine. This was his domain, his kingdom, and he loved it.

The big man stretched out and lazily scratched his sack, feeling his bull-sized balls roll against his fingers through the polyester tan uniform slacks that gripped his big ass and package like a glove. His cock stood out like a Fletcher's corn dog from the State Fair in the thin pants, like a goddamn bratwurst with a fat mushroom at the top. He squeezed his cock and felt it grow thicker in his hand. The crisp white t-shirt under his uniform shirt covered a thick mat of chestnut brown hair that carpeted his barrel chest and beer gut that drifted over the leather Sam Brown gun belt. He patted his belly and grinned. Not too bad for forty-five, he thought. He was stronger than an ox and fast as lightning on his feet if he ever had to chase someone, which was pretty much never, these days. His hand bumped against his Glock sidearm. He tried to remember the last time he had to unholster his weapon except at the firing range. Things like that didn't happen a lot in Lone Pine.

The village of Lone Pine was known for three things: fried pies, the Lone Pine Okra Fest in September, and speed traps. The three mile stretch of Hwy 69 that ran east–west through the city limits was posted with plenty of signs reminding travelers of the 25 mph speed limit. The short school zone was marked at 20 mph. The place was notorious for absolute rigidity in regards to the speed limits and tickets were handed out like Halloween treats to the offenders. Sheriff Givens was the municipality's one and only law enforcement officer. He and his good friend, Judge Ezekiel Crow, held court once a week for the few idiots that attempted to talk their way out of their speeding ticket. They had a snowball's chance in hell of getting out of it. In fact, the court was just as likely to slap on additional sanctions for wasting their time when visitors attempted it.

Arlo and the traffic citations accounted for almost fifty percent of the annual revenue for the small town, sometimes even more. The high school kids that learned to drive were particularly careful to not break the rules, not wanting to face the wrath and monetary punishments. In fact, it was so rare to have an incident involving the youth of the town, Arlo rarely thought about it at all. No, the main preys that fell into his speed trap were college students headed to and from Stephen F. Austin University in Nacogdoches, and out of state drivers from Louisiana and Arkansas that were foolish enough to not believe the speed signs. They rarely made the same mistake twice. It was told that many in the area would go out of their way and take other routes to complete their travel to avoid the traps. It mattered very little to Arlo. Like a Venus fly-trap, he sat in his patrol truck and simply waited. In no time at all, another juicy fly would spring the jaws of the trap shut. They could cry and complain all they wanted and he would still write the ticket, especially to the women. In fact, nothing made him angrier than a woman who tried to use her gender or femininity to try and get out of the ticket. Over the years, he had been flashed, bribed, and threatened. He had watched women dissolve into tears, put on lipstick, slide a skirt up so high you could see her twat and he would snarl and hike the fine up ten percent more.

It was a different story with the men and boys. He liked the smart-ass ones, relished the fools who actually thought they could intimidate him, and most of all, loved the meek ones who were willing to do anything… absolutely anything to get out of the ticket. Sometimes, they would make an offer themselves, much to Arlo's delight. Other times if he felt like it, he would offer them a chance to get out of the fine. The rush was in seeing how they would react: shock, embarrassment, anger, humiliation. It was all part of the game and part of his joy in his job. Arlo felt his cock stir as he considered all the ways he had mitigated those tickets over the past few years. This was rural Texas. There were no fucking video cameras or audio recordings. He didn't even have a local dispatch to call back to. His radio calls were monitored all the way over in Greenville. There was no back up. He was the law, he and his Glock and his badge and it had proven to be more than enough to take care of him for years. He didn't profile either. He stopped every color, race, gender, and ethnicity and treated them all the same, like the shits they were for speeding like fuck through his town.

Arlo had tried to make his marriage work for the past fifteen years and finally admitted it was hopeless. He was gone so much and his wife was always angry and distant. She resented the hell out of him being so absent and tired. When he found out she was fucking some bubba from Turnbull, he got so mad he thought about killing the guy. But in the end, he figured he had done him a big favor. It was easy to slide out of a loveless marriage and let it be all Justine's fault. The one successful part of his sad marriage was his three boys. Colt was fifteen, Jackson was thirteen, and Gunner was ten. All three were big boys, thick, blond, muscled, tough, and but with a sweet side that Arlo loved. When the boys stayed with him on weekends off, they had a blast. Half the time, the youngest ones would fall asleep in Arlo's big king-sized bed. Sometimes, Colt would be in there too. He would lay awake and watch them and feel the pride in his heart soar. The two oldest boys had man-sized dicks already with a thick crop of fur around their gonads and pits. Gunner was still small and smooth, but sometimes Arlo thought his baby might just end up bigger and hairier than the older boys he was changing so fast. Unlike the way his old man had told him absolutely nothing about sex, he made sure his boys understood their bodies and encouraged them to masturbate as often as they wanted. The horned up Givens brothers took him at his word and ended up jacking off so much his ex-wife called almost monthly to complain her wash cloths and hand towels were constantly found under their beds, crusted and stiff with boy batter.

Arlo just listened and replied, "Boys will be boys. They ain't hurtin' no one Justine. Better to squirt off on your towels than in some trailer trash teen twat." Usually, the phone would hang up at that point and he would howl in laughter.

These days, the idea of hooking up with another woman didn't fill him with much excitement or arousal. He knew it was unfair to only focus on the bad parts, but damn, she was such a harpy. Maybe someday he would find a nice lady and try it again. But for now, he had found another outlet for his libido and it was working just fine.

The whine of the radar gun woke Arlo from his daydream and he locked in like a hawk on the display.

"47 in a 25. Fuck me sideways, I love my job." Arlo flipped on the red and blues and burned out of his hideaway.

If you enjoyed this sample then look for **Bad Sheriff**.

# Our First Meeting

## The Notebook

D.D. WATSON

He searched for shelter having no clue where to turn. Exposed to the world and vulnerable, skin damp and sprinkled with dirt from running through the woods.

The forest was dense and had no visible trails; the sun was going down and the entwined branches blocked out what little light he had. Tears welled in his eyes, but he fought them back refusing to show any form of weakness.

He found shelter in a cave that was for now, his only refuge; he fled from his captors or maybe; they let him escape? He wrapped his arms around his shivering body as he kneeled down to the ground exhausted from the run he had to endure on barefoot. His body screamed from the torments; only moments ago inflicted on him...

\*\*\*

Arian Taylor-Kinney, nicknamed Rin by his fathers, scribbled hastily in his notebook the story that burned in his head. A college student with brilliant soft golden-brown eyes, long auburn hair that shaped his soft face and seemed to obey as it drifts across his magnet eyes when he read or smiled with his curvy lips. His trim built helped draped his clothing that usually was just tee shirts and jeans. Arian hasn't had experience in relationships, sexual or monogamy. He was homeschooled by his father from pre-school to the last day of high school.

When entering college he wasn't as overwhelmed with his academics as he and his parents predicted, socializing was a bit different, but not problematic he has been to different groups where he'd made friends growing up, dance, soccer, swimming, and theater.

During his first semester he mostly focused on finding his classes, having to share his views in front of strangers, appointments, lectures, and due dates.

He bypassed moving into the dorms something his fathers disapproved. Arian reasoned that they lived close to the campus and that he would make friends just as easy commuting back and forward and that it would just be a waste of money.

As he settled into his second semester, he began to notice other people who were interested in him, males and females. Arian didn't want to be distracted from his studies, so he made friendships but nothing more. To tame the growing urges he had from the offers he was receiving from his classmates, mainly the males, he continued a method he performed back in high school to write his desires down in spiral notebooks.

The fantasies detail in location, positions; the men involved and the level of heat they were performing. Arian spilled his darkest, purest desires out on the line paper and what started with one notebook turned into more. He even came across a muse that seemed unreal, but he did become Arian's star player in most of his fantasies.

Sitting outside was a joy for him because during his younger days, and on nice weather his father performed a few of his lessons at the park or in their backyard. On this one particular day, Arian enjoyed relaxing alone on a bench under the shade of trees while writing and watching passerbyers.

"Hey Arian," said a tall blonde male who sat beside him as if he was a close friend. His physique was impressive showing through his close-fitting tank top and shorts as he put his arm behind Arian's shoulders resting it on the bench. Staring at the brawny arm, Arian wondered if he could dodge it—if his interloper decides to embrace him.

"Sorry, do I know you?" he asked leaning forward closing his notebook and grasping it firmly in his lap.

"Sure you do— Peter we have the same English class, Professor Law?" he smiled a familiar smile that Arian's become accustomed to. The same grin that said more behind it than it presented. His hand dropped to Arian's upper back, he tensed up and tried to shift away.

"I'm sorry I'm pretty sure I would remember you." Peter leaned closer placing his free palm on top of Arian's whom gripped his notebook even tighter.

"Well to be honest you always had your head in a book or writing something in that notebook but I did make it my business to sit nearby you and ask for a pencil."

"That was you?"

"Yes and it hurts my feelings that you don't remember me."

"Sorry, Professor Law had a lot of notes to take down, and he had asked me to use my notes as a class reference," Arian lied.

"Well, you can make it up to me." His fingers slid down Arian's spin sending heated tension throughout his skin.

"I can?" Arian shifted again and managed stop the message the sensation was sending to his cock.

"Dinner at my place," said Peter, who ignored Arian's evading.

"Your place?"

"Yeah, I have an apartment, my parents' ideal to help me study," he said looking Arian over intently as he moved his fingers from his back to reach around and touch his face.

"Is it helping?" Arian asked turning his face to avoid Peter's touch on his cheek only to get caught locking eyes with his green orbs. Peter managed to catch Arian's chin and hold his gaze.

"Well, why don't you come over with your notes and you can test me?"

"Well I—"

Just before Arian was about to turn him down a male student ran up to them grabbing Peter's arm.

"Peter you need to come quick."

"Not now Sam, I'm busy," he snapped keeping his attention on Arian.

"But your car." That did it; Peter leaped from the bench and fixated his full concentration on Sam.

"What about my car?"

"All the tires are missing."

"What?!"

"Also the engine."

"Are you kidding me?"

"Go see for yourself."

Peter darting away, Sam remained behind as Peter raced off and turned to Arian, who was standing collecting his things to head to class.

"Where you headed?" asked Sam. Arian looked at him with a puzzled look.

"To class."

"Aren't you concerned about Peter's car?"

"It's none of my business."

"That's not what I saw a moment ago you two looked quite comfy."

Arian wasn't skilled in relationships but did know when someone was jealous.

"Look, I scarcely knew Peter until now so whatever—this is," he gestured with his hand. "He's all yours."

"Damn right he is. I see what you do to men," he snapped, stomping off.

"What did he mean by that?" thought Arian, as he walked to his next class.

A young male watched the scene with full concentration as if he was watching a play. He held a can of unopened soda between his ring-covered fingers. As Arian walked away, Sam approached him.

"All better?" he asked taking the soda from him.

"Yeah thanks, I owe you."

"So you'll cover for me at work on Saturday?"

"Can do."

"Thanks Cross you're a life saver," he said popping the cap and taking a deep swallow.

"No, you are," replied Cross, gathering his messenger bag that strangely resembled Arian's that Sam noticed.

"Hey, I know it's none of my business but if you like him then just tell him."

"I couldn't handle the rejection."

"Cross you're beautiful, if you weren't so into him I'd ask you out."

"But I am into him and—I would like to handle it in my way."

If you enjoyed this sample then look for <u>**Our First Meeting**</u>.

**WANT FREE COPIES OF MY BOOKS?**
Just visit my blog and download free copies of my books:
http://gideon-elliot.awesomeauthors.org/gideon-elliot/

www.ingramcontent.com/pod-product-compliance
Lightning Source LLC
Chambersburg PA
CBHW071321130626
46556CB00004B/1698